THE
ADVENTURES
OF
ARTIE AND ZAC

JUDEH SIMON

To my family,

you opened my eyes to a magical everyday world.

When I was younger, my dad often shared stories of his mysterious journeys. He spoke endlessly about all the amazing adventures he went on before I was born – but the thing is, the stuff he talked about couldn't possibly be real...Talking dragons? ...Pixies? ...Magic? I may have believed it all when I was in preschool, but I'm much older now. I don't think such things really exist.

My name is Zac. I am eight years old. I live with my dad in a *mostly* quiet neighborhood in San Francisco. The neighbors *rarely* complain about all the loud noises from inside our garage.

Dad is an inventor. He spends most of his days, and some nights, in our garage, hammering, sawing, drilling, bolting and hammering some more.

I mostly go to school. My favorite subject is recess. I also like lunchtime. It's like recess but there's food! My least favorite subject is math. Luckily, I won't have to worry about math for some time now because today was the last day of school.

Dad and I are about to embark on a summer long vacation to some secret place he won't tell me about.

My dad secretly planned our vacation during the school year, while I attended school. He worked diligently from his workshop in our garage…where I wasn't allowed.

"By the wizard's great ear wax, we're all packed!" said dad. He walked outside carrying his belongings in a box.

"Are you all done cleaning up your room?" he added.

"Almost done," I answered.

I looked around my room one last time. All my school books were neatly put away on my shelves. My skateboard, baseball bat and art supplies were all tucked away, not so neatly, under my bed.

I grabbed my travel backpack and ran outside to meet up with dad. I found him in our driveway, just standing there.

"Where's our ride?" I asked.

"The ride? The ride…oh yes, it's inside the garage," he replied.

"Are we driving there?" I added.

"Not quite - not if I can help it," answered dad. "I've been working on our transport in my spare time."

He clicked the garage door opener.

"Wait here," he said, "the pixies don't like uninvited visitors."

Dad didn't always make sense. I learned to just go with the flow whenever he mentioned pixies, wizards or dragons.

The garage door lifted all the way up. He went inside and came back out a few minutes later, pulling a huge wicker basket with some ropes dragging behind it.

"I present to you…our ride," he said. "Help me move it to the sidewalk."

I hurried to help, but I was still confused as to how a simple wicker basket was going to be our ride.

We pulled the basket out front. The ropes attached to it were dragging a deflated red balloon.

"You built a hot air balloon!" I shouted, "we're traveling in a hot air balloon!?!?"

"Don't worry," said dad, "the pixies assured me it's perfectly safe and functional."

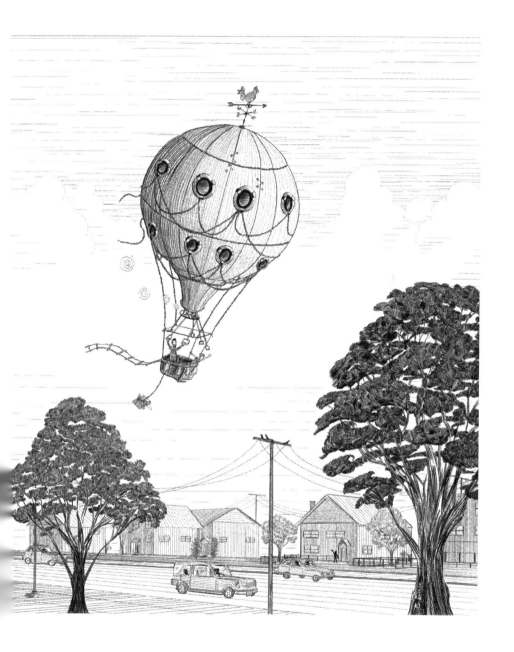

As crazy as it may seem, dad's inventions always work. One time, he built a boat out of milk cartons and it successfully carried us across a lake.

We finished loading our belongings into the basket and we jumped in. Dad fired up the burners. The hot air started to fill the envelope. The balloon floated up as it filled with air. Our basket started to float up as well.

Some of the neighbors ran to their windows to get a closer look at the humongous machine in front of our garage.

I waved at them awkwardly while neighborhood dogs barked excitedly at all the commotion.

"Hold on to something," said dad, "it's about to get shakier than the gusts of fate."

We rose higher. I held on to the edge of the basket and looked down. Everything got smaller and smaller.

Dad maneuvered us up and away from the houses and trees.

We eventually cleared all the structures. Dad reached into his pocket and pulled out a glowing compass. He held it tightly in the palm of his hand.

"Winds of dragon don't fail me now," he muttered, and quickly followed up with a confident tone: "The winds at this elevation are blowing south - they will push us in the precise direction."

The hot air balloon moved gently through the clear blue skies. Dad pocketed the compass before I could take a closer look at it.

Suddenly, an unexpected gust of wind pushed us right into a fog bank.

"AHHH…" I yelled. "I can't see anything through this thick fog!"

Dad remained calm and reached into his pocket one more time. He pulled out his compass again. The compass flickered brighter and brighter until a beam of light burst out from it. The light beam cut through the thick fog, acting as a beacon, guiding us in the right direction.

"No need to worry," said dad. "This is just like that one time at the sea of echoes. We'll clear through it in no time!"

"Dad, where did you get that thing?" I was looking at the compass still in his hand.

"It was a gift from a knight," he replied.

The skies turned blue again.

"We're in the clear," said dad.

"Looks like we're flying over some woods," I said.

"Time to bring us down," he replied.

We landed the balloon by a field of wildflowers at the edge of the woods. It wasn't the smoothest of landings. We survived.

"Our home for the summer is up ahead," said dad.

"My friend," dad pointed to an old gray castle across the wildflower field. "She'll meet us by the drawbridge!"

We climbed out of the basket, stretched our legs and started walking towards the fortress.

The castle looked rather timeworn. Claw marks stood out along one side, as if a huge animal had taken a swing at it. One of the walls was covered in soot. Upon closer inspection, it appeared to be fire damage and grime.

"Dad," I hesitated before continuing, "Who lives here?"

"It's a surprise," said dad with a smirk. "Besides, she doesn't really live in the castle. No, she wouldn't fit through the door. She just likes to hang out in the area."

Suddenly, I felt strong gusts of wind blowing through my hair.

"She's here," cried dad with an overdramatic tone, as he announced her arrival.

I craned my neck to look up. A massive dragon hovered above us. Our landlady lowered herself down, while gently flapping her bat-like wings. She landed right in front of us.

"Good to see you again Esmeralda," said dad.

"You too, old friend," said the dragon.

I stood there in disbelief. My jaw was probably open all the way. A huge talking dragon stood in front of me.

"Esmeralda is moving to the icy mountains to have her babies," said dad. "I offered to house sit for her through the summer until she comes back."

I don't quite remember how long the dragon was there. They talked for what felt like hours, or maybe it was just minutes. I just stood there, staring at the incredible dragon in front of me.

Our summer vacation was off to a great start! The shock of seeing a real life dragon eventually wore off. I spent most of my days exploring the castle's secret passageways and discovering hidden rooms. Dad spent long hours bouncing between the library and his study. We were both determined to learn as much as we could about this place and its history.

"This morning, I'm going to explore the castle's tower," I told dad.

"*Mmmhh*," grunted dad, without looking up from his book. He clearly has not had his morning coffee yet.

I ran down the hall towards the stairwell, but before I could make it up the stairs, my attention was drawn towards a large blow horn resting on a stand. I've seen these things before in museums. This one was carved from a very large animal's horn.

I picked it up. I blew into the mouthpiece. It produced a loud, shrieking sound that echoed through the chamber. It was as if somebody screamed into a hundred megaphones at once.

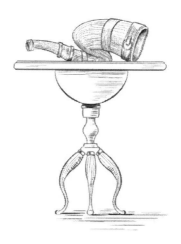

I quickly threw the horn back on its stand and covered my ears. Once the ringing in my ears stopped, I backed away from the horn and headed up the stairs towards the castle's tower.

At the top of the stairwell stood a huge mirror partially covered with a dark cloth. It was almost as tall as the ceiling. I removed the cloth cover.

"AHHH," my distorted reflection caught me off guard. The mirror was warped in such a way that made me look like a giant.

After my initial shock wore off, I started practicing my ninja moves in front of the mirror. Giant-me looked very strong and imposing.

I was still posturing in front of the mirror when I heard dad's footsteps. He was marching down the hall towards the kitchen.

I ran downstairs to remind him about the chickens.

"Dad," I shouted.

"MORE CO-FFEE," he groaned in his dry morning voice.

A flock of wild chickens had moved into our kitchen shortly after we arrived. Possibly due to all the grains we endlessly dropped on the kitchen floor. Or maybe they just liked the company.

"Don't forget, the chickens are in the kitchen..." I started to warn him, but before I could finish, I heard a loud CRASH, followed by a TUMBLE, and finally a SPLAT.

Dad most likely startled the chickens again. This in turn startled him, causing him to trip and fall. This is becoming a daily incident.

"The chickens are safe," yelled dad from behind the kitchen doors. "I'm ok too."

They were very stubborn chickens. It took dad a while to figure out how to get rid of them. There was a lot of trial and error involved, but he finally found a recipe in one of the library's magic books.

Trinket Stew, he called it. It smelled awful. But the smell of it was the only thing that kept the chickens away.

"Patient old monk, be proud! I'm going to prepare some trinket stew," exclaimed dad. "Want to assist a rookie magician?"

"No way," I said.

I covered my nose to remind dad that I couldn't stand the smell of his stew.

"I'm going to play outside," I shouted.

I quickly left the castle.

I didn't see the point of preparing the trinket stew anyways. The chickens would just come back the next day and the whole ritual would start all over again.

Outside, wildflowers and tall grasses covered the fields. It was obviously Esmeralda's favorite spot. Her many footprints formed giant craters across the land. This was certainly the best place to be when the castle smelled of trinket stew.

"Look out below," I yelled as I ran towards one of the footprints.

I jumped up and landed inside its crater.

"ROOOAK," croaked a handful of startled frogs.

They quickly jumped out of the muddy footprint and headed towards the ponds.

"I'm sorry if I scared you," I apologized.

I climbed out of the footprint, wiped the mud from my shoes against the grass, and made my way to a nearby cottage.

At the cottage, tied to one of the posts, I found my newest companion.

"Alex!" I yelled with excitement.

Alex is my mechanical steed. He's one of dad's newest inventions.

Dad built Alex using parts from a hobby-horse, an old bicycle and some metal gears.

"Let's go for a ride," I said as I took the reins.

I climbed on and started pedaling. The wheels between his legs started to turn, and off we went.

We rode all the way to the edge of the woods, leaving a trail of dust behind us. We stopped for a couple of minutes to catch our breath.

A sound startled me.

"OOOUUWW," the mysterious voice cried repeatedly from within the woods.

"What sad howls," I whispered. "What could be causing them?"

I tied Alex to a nearby tree, "Someone may need help!"

I walked towards the woods, in the direction of the howls.

I entered the woods.

The tree canopy was thick. Very little sunlight reached the ground, but my eyes gradually adjusted to the dark.

I made my way through tangled branches and spider webs.

"This way," said a quiet voice near my ear.

"Hurry," said another.

"Who *are* you?" I asked. "*Where* are you?"

I looked around but couldn't see anyone.

"Here," called one of the voices. "We're forest pixies."

She fluttered her wings and moved closer to me.

"You're real!" I shouted with glee. "Dad always talks about you!"

Seeing dad's famed pixies confirmed all his stories were true.

"Nice to make your acquaintance, Zac!" said the first pixie. "We've heard so much about you."

More and more pixies flew towards me and joined their group. The woods filled with small bright lights.

"This is amazing," I said, as I briefly stopped to watch the incredible light show above me.

"He needs your help," said one of the pixies. "Follow us."

I followed the tiny lights through the tangled branches.

"Thank you for lighting the way," I said. "Is somebody in trouble?"

"Hurry," said the pixies as they flew faster.

I ran behind them. We reached the entrance to a cave.

"Inside," said the pixies, before scattering into the tree tops.

The sad howls came from inside the cave.

21

Before going in, I picked up a broken branch from a nearby tree. "This should help in case I run into any trouble."

Quietly, I snuck inside the cave. Fire torches lined the walls. I pulled a torch off its bracket and took it with me to help light the way.

Armed with my fighting stick and my shiny light, I felt very prepared to journey deeper.

Empty bird cages lay scattered across the floor.

"This is strange," I whispered.

Suddenly, I heard the howling again. This time, much louder.

Just around the corner, I found the source of the cries.

A cat, trapped inside one of the cages. He had short black fur and big yellow eyes. His front paws were big and fluffy.

"Your assistance would be greatly appreciated!" said the cat, "that is, please help me get out of this cage."

"You talk!" I yelled, no longer surprised by such things.

"Only when there's something worth saying," answered the cat, amused with his own sly reply.

"My name is Artie," he continued, "Artie - the cat."

"I'm Zac," I answered, "Zac…the boy. You have the biggest paws I have ever seen on a cat."

"I'm a polydactyl cat," said Artie, "that is, I have more toes than the usual. We are exceptionally rare and special."

He raised one of his paws so I could take a closer look. It had six toes on it. The extra toes made his paws look like mittens.

I looked around for a key to open the lock, but there were none to be found.

I put my weapon and torch down on the ground and tried forcing the cage door open with my hands, but it was made of steel. It would not open, no matter how hard I pulled.

"Why are you inside this cage?" I asked.

"A goblin locked me up," said Artie. "He wants to keep me here as his prisoner. He kept mumbling something about his lucky black cat."

"That's terrible," I replied. Where is he now?"

"Off to hunt for more creatures to imprison," Artie guessed. "The key to the cage is on the shelf by the cauldron."

He wedged his fluffy paw between the bars and pointed at a shelf behind me.

Following the cat's gesture, I turned around.

I immediately found the shelf. It was next to a big pot with boiling water, sitting on top of an open fire.

I ran to the shelf and picked up the cluster of keys. They were held together by a small metal ring.

"A key for every cage," I assumed.

I quickly found the correct key and unlocked the door. Artie jumped out and licked me on the cheek. It was his way of showing gratitude.

As we started to make our way out of the cave, we heard the sound of feet stomping.

"Oh no," I said. "It looks like the goblin has returned. We are trapped inside."

We couldn't leave the cave with the goblin blocking the entrance. I needed a plan.

What could I do to chase the goblin away? I focused for a few seconds until I remembered the wild chickens and dad's awful-smelling trinket stew. It was powerful enough to drive the stubborn chickens out of the kitchen.

If I cooked the stew inside this cave, I thought, it would smell so bad that the goblin would have no choice but to flee the stench. It would give us a moment to escape while he was away.

"We must use that cauldron to make trinket stew!" I announced.

I had watched dad prepare his stew in the past. I just needed to remember the list of ingredients.

I tapped my finger on my forehead a few times in an attempt to nudge my memory. Finally, the recipe came back to me: "Dirty dishes and smelly socks, rotten veggies and wooden blocks. A frog's old luggage and borrowed cabbage, stir them up in boiling water, blow on the fire and make it hotter."

"That doesn't even make any sense," said Artie.

"Trust me," I said. "This stuff works!"

We diligently started searching for ingredients among the rubbish.

There were plenty of dirty dishes everywhere. Our host clearly didn't believe in cleaning up after himself. We gently dropped a few plates into the cauldron.

My socks were kind of smelly. I *had been* wearing them on my feet for a very long time that day. I quickly took one off and tossed it into the mix.

Luckily, there were lots of rotten vegetables, including

cabbage, scattered all over the floor. We borrowed some.

The remaining ingredients, a wooden block and a frog's old luggage, were a bit harder to find. One of the stools in the cave had wooden blocks for legs. I removed one of them and added it to the stew.

"Where are we going to find a frog's old luggage?" I asked. "I met a couple of frogs earlier today, but they had no luggage at all."

"We could use *my* luggage" said Artie.

"You…have luggage?" I said with a puzzled look on my face.

"I use it to carry my catnip when I travel," said the cat. "I don't see any traveling frogs around here, so *my* luggage will have to do."

We added Artie's luggage to our trinket stew, puckered our lips, and blew gently against the flames.

"Now we wait," I said.

At first, nothing happened, but after a few minutes, the most awful, stinky, terrible smell started coming out of the cauldron.

I held both my hands up to my face and covered my nose. Artie only needed one of his big paws to cover his snout.

The smell traveled to where the goblin was resting.

"Ewwww!!" screeched the goblin. "What a foul terrible smell this is!" He left the cave.

"This is our chance to get out of here," I said.

We quickly ran out of the cave and made our way back to the woods.

I was curious. I wanted to take a clear look at the goblin before leaving, so we hid behind some trees and waited for him to return.

To my surprise, the creature came back rather quickly. The smell of *our* stew was fading a lot faster than my dad's usual stuff.

"I knew we needed a frog's old luggage!" I said. "Cat's luggage just doesn't carry the smell that long," I added, realizing that I was beginning to sound like dad.

Our adversary stood in front of the cave. I was finally able to get my first clear look at him.

He was an awkward looking thing indeed. He wasn't much taller than a boy. His bare feet, were much bigger than what is usually needed for such a small body. His clothes were old and torn. He had skinny long arms that stretched almost all the way to his feet.

His face was made up of an oversized nose with two tiny eyes on each side of it. His large ears probably granted him very good hearing.

Just then, the goblin looked in my direction as if listening for something.

A sound came from Artie.

"PRRR," He was rubbing his whiskers on my leg and purring very loudly. The goblin's attention was definitely drawn towards the loud purring sounds.

"Artie," I whispered, "stop purring right now."

It was too late. The goblin noticed us. He started running towards us.

"RUN, ARTIE! RUN!"

We both ran as fast as we could through the dark woods, in the direction of our castle. The goblin chased us. His big feet signaled his location with every loud stomp.

As we exited the woods, we reunited with Alex, my hobby-horse, who was waiting to carry us back to safety. I quickly untied his reins.

We started riding through the wildflower fields, towards our castle.

Artie ran next to me. His tiny feet were not fast enough to outrun the goblin.

I steered Alex closer and reached down with my free hand. I picked Artie up and threw him over my shoulder. He started purring again.

"Hang on Artie," I cried. "We're almost there!"

The castle came into view.

As we got closer, the drawbridge lowered. Dad walked intently across the bridge, towards us.

Meanwhile, the goblin's stomping sounds got louder and louder. He was getting closer. We were within his reach.

Dad revealed a pot he had been hiding behind himself. He flung its contents past me, high into the air, and right onto the goblin. The lumpy stew knocked the creature down to the ground and ended his stampede.

"Have some trinket stew!" yelled dad.

"YES!" I shouted.

With dad's well-timed arrival, we were now safe.

I was relieved and grateful.

"GAHH…" mumbled the goblin as he tried to stand up again. "What terrible spell is this!?"

He tried to stand, but the stew's gooey mush weighed him down.

Realizing that he was now outnumbered, he clumsily crawled back into the woods, muttering something about revenge.

"That will teach him to come after my boy," said dad.

"How did you know we were in trouble?" I asked.

"The forest pixies and I go way back! They're always watching, always listening…" he started to drift off, but then composed himself and declared: "they came to warn me."

I threw my arms around dad and gave him a big hug.

"Now tell me," he continued, "is your new friend staying for dinner?"

By late summer, the woods completely transformed. Gone was the dense tree canopy. Leaves continuously dropped to the ground. They formed a carpet of reds and yellows at the base of each trunk.

Artie and I walked along the edge of the woods collecting wood for our fireplace. I happily pushed a wheelbarrow while Artie jumped randomly behind me.

"What are you doing?" I asked, as Artie dove into a huge pile of leaves.

"It appears I spotted a rodent," he replied. "That is, I thought I saw a mouse."

"Right," I said with a cynical smile. "You just can't pass up the opportunity to pounce into a huge pile of leaves. I understand."

Artie had gotten so plump from my dad's constant cooking, that even if he *did* see a mouse, he'd be too sluggish to do anything about it.

He continued to play in his pile of leaves while I collected more wood for the fireplace.

Suddenly, from deep within the woods, a small light headed my way.

"Pixies," I said softly.

"He's coming," said one of the pixies.

"He wants his thing," said another pixie, pointing at Artie.

"Pardon me," said Artie "I'm nobody's thing. I belong to me."

"He wants his lucky cat," said the first pixie.

"He's gathered his army," a third pixie continued, "you won't fare as well against this many goblins."

"Be warned," said the second one.

Pixies regularly finished each other's sentences. This made it hard to focus during our conversations.

"They will be here in the morning," said the first pixie.

"Thank you for letting us know," I said.

The pixies quickly flew up and disappeared into the tree tops.

Artie and I hurriedly ran back home. We found dad diligently reading in his study.

"Lizard's breath," he mumbled. "How am I supposed to collect lizard's breath?"

Dad looked up at us. He could see from the expression on our faces that something was wrong. He quickly put his book down and ran towards us.

We shared with him what the pixies told us, and that we only had one night to prepare for the return of the goblin.

"No need to worry," said dad. "Use this castle, use the tools within it and the knowledge you have gathered to defend us from the goblins."

Artie and I did exactly what my dad told us to do. We devised a plan, and we prepared to defend our home from the invading army.

The next morning, I woke up early and went up to the castle's tower. I wanted to spot the goblin army as soon as it made its way out of the woods. Artie and dad soon joined me by the tower's window.

Moments later, the first of the goblins burst through the shrubs. It was the leader of the pack. I remembered his awkwardly big feet and long arms. We hadn't had such a good encounter the last time we met. I hoped our first meeting would also be our last. No such luck.

He spotted me in the tower's window.

"I WANT MY THING BACK," he cried.

His voice echoed through the halls of the castle. I have to admit, I was scared. He was much angrier this time.

I instinctively hid away from sight.

I took a deep breath, calmed my fears and looked out the window again. This time, I saw a pack of angry goblins riding on the backs of beasts that looked like oversized pigs.

"Wild warthogs," explained dad, as he joined me at the window, "they're friendly creatures, but can be quite hostile when provoked."

Horned saddles and leather straps made them look much more intimidating.

Dad pulled us close to him and said: "Remember: goblins are gullible and clumsy. They scare easily. And *you* have a plan."

We headed down to the castle's drawbridge. Dad lowered it. Artie and I stood in the middle of the entryway. Our faces were marked with our best courageous expressions.

"Go back to your homes," I yelled. "Artie is nobody's property. He is his own person and he chooses to stay here, with us."

"HE IS MINE," yelled the goblin.

"You have been warned," I continued, "we are powerful wizards."

"Yes, I remember," said the goblin, "your stinky spells are no match against all of us. And we know the dragon is away. Nothing here will protect you."

He tugged at the straps in his hands forcefully, and promptly, his warthog started charging towards us.

The other goblins followed.

Artie and I ran towards the goblin pack. As I ran, I put my hand in my pocket and pulled out an old gemstone. Just a random blue rock I found on one of my walks. I held it up high so all the goblins could see it. "With this gem… I summon the rain of *toxic* frogs."

Just then, Artie jumped inside one of the dragon footprints by the ponds and I ran through a different footprint. An army of disoriented and alarmed frogs jumped out of their hiding places. They leaped in every direction and created panic among the goblins.

"Sorry guys," I quietly apologized to the frogs.

The confusion and panic created by the flight of frogs knocked the goblins off their mounts.

The warthogs, having no quarrel with us, ran back towards the woods. I spotted a couple of the ever-helpful pixies approaching the warthogs and watched them remove the horrible saddles off their backs.

"GAAAHH," cried one of the goblins who had been struck by a frog. "I've been poisoned."

"Leave now," I repeated.

Some of them *did* leave. They scattered in every direction while repeatedly wiping at their faces and bodies, believing themselves poisoned by the frogs.

To this first group of goblins, it was enough excitement for one day.

The rest of the goblins, however, stayed. They were not as easily persuaded to abandon their hunt.

"I will not leave here without my thing," said the goblin leader.

"Then you leave me no choice," I replied. "I will summon the giant chickens, the great defenders of this land."

I pointed to one of the dragon footprints in the mud and trusted that the goblins would mistake them for giant chicken claw prints.

"Look for yourselves," I gestured.

Fear and hesitation marked the goblins' faces. Some took a few steps back while others held their ground, as if to demand more proof.

"Unchain the giant chickens," I continued.

The loud sounds came first: CLUCK. CLUCK. COO. COO. FLAP. FLAP. FLAP.

Then, from behind the castle, the tallest, most gigantic chickens ever imagined appeared and started marching towards us.

The blow horn and oversized mirror did the trick!

While Artie and I performed our first wave of tricks, dad managed to march the chickens right onto our prepared stage. The blow horn amplified the chicken's cooing noises, while the mirror made them look like giants.

"By the keepers of the great chickens, it worked," I said. Now I was definitely sounding like dad.

The remaining goblins took one look at the giant chickens reflected in the mirror and quickly started to retreat. They ran back into the woods, clumsily stumbling over each other. Their leader tried holding a few of them in position to no avail.

The goblin leader, who was now outnumbered, turned around and joined them inside the woods.

"They'll think twice before coming here again," said dad. "You both did a great job! I'm proud of the two of you. Your plan drove the goblins away."

The three of us watched as the last of the goblins disappeared into the shadows.

The chickens were already on their way back to the kitchen.

Dad went back inside.

Artie and I stayed outside a little bit longer. We wanted to be certain that the danger was really over.

"Trouble has floated away," said Artie, "that is, it looks safe to go back inside."

"Yeah," I sighed.

Artie's suggestion of things floating away reminded me of the hot air balloon.

"What might be troubling you?" asked Artie.

"Summer break is almost over." I answered. "We have to return to San Francisco soon."

On our last day of vacation, we stood in front of the castle; dad, Artie and I. Our hot air balloon stood ready to fly us back to San Francisco. Our belongings were packed away inside the basket. The red balloon filled with air.

"Thus concludes our adventure!" said dad.

"I wish we didn't have to go," I grumbled.

I had grown fond of this place. I will miss the castle, with its artifacts and secret rooms. I will miss the woods and the pixies. I will even miss the chickens.

"Gaze upwards," cried Artie, "that is, she returns!"

Esmeralda flew across the orange afternoon sky, followed by her five baby dragons.

They all landed in the wildflower fields in front of the castle. Their heavy bodies made their feet sink slightly into the mud, creating fresh new hollows for the frogs to inhabit.

Dad and Esmeralda said their goodbyes.

Saying goodbye to good friends is never easy, especially when you won't see them again for a very long time.

Fortunately, Artie and I didn't have to say such goodbyes today.

"These games of video and the iced cream, I am not familiar with," said Artie. "I am very much looking forward to licking the cream of ice when we get back to your home."

"Then you're in for a true adventure, my friend!" I replied. "And it is *our* home now."

Having grown as fond of me as I of him, Artie decided to come back to San Francisco with us.

He promised not to speak in front of any other humans.

As for me, after surviving this adventure, I never doubted dad's stories ever again.

ABOUT THE AUTHOR

JUDEH SIMON picks up dirty socks …a lot. He makes stew, cleans dirty dishes and wakes at random hours of the night to quiet down a vocalizing cat. A former industrial engineer and video game artist, he reliably maintains one foot set in this world and the other in the realm of imagination. His passion for storytelling never subsides. He managed to write and illustrate this book you are holding. He is so very tired.

Made in the USA
Coppell, TX
13 October 2020